Coloring Book for Adults

Fairy Tales

Coloring Book

I0530898

MantraCraft

This Coloring Book belongs to:

_____

_____

_____

_____

Color Test Page

www.ingramcontent.com/pod-product-compliance
Lightning Source LLC
Chambersburg PA
CBHW082250120626
46555CB00009B/3029